The Little Girl and the Tiny Doll

Edward Ardizzone was born in 1900, the eldest of five children. He went to evening classes at the Westminster School of Art and became a professional painter. Several of his pictures have been bought by the Tate Gallery. During World War II he was one of the six official war artists. He illustrated more than 200 books and was awarded the Kate Greenaway Medal for *Tim All Alone*. He was awarded the CBE in 1971 and died in 1979.

Aingelda Ardizzone lives in Kent. When she told this story to her children, she was persuaded by her father-in-law, Edward Ardizzone, to write it down. What was more he offered to illustrate it! Now it is read to her grandchildren.

Aingelda studied at the Slade School of Fine Art and is a painter. A later story, *The Night Ride*, is also illustrated by Edward Ardizzone.

Edward and Aingelda Ardizzone

The Little Girl and the Tiny Doll

PUFFIN

PUFFIN BOOKS

Published by the Penguin Group
Penguin Books Ltd, 80 Strand, London WC2R 0RL, England
Penguin Group (USA) Inc., 375 Hudson Street, New York, New York 10014, USA
Penguin Group (Canada), 90 Eglinton Avenue East, Suite 700, Toronto, Ontario, Canada M4P 2Y3
(a division of Pearson Penguin Canada Inc.)
Penguin Ireland, 25 St Stephen's Green, Dublin 2, Ireland (a division of Penguin Books Ltd)
Penguin Group (Australia), 250 Camberwell Road, Camberwell, Victoria 3124, Australia
(a division of Pearson Australia Group Pty Ltd)
Penguin Books India Pvt Ltd, 11 Community Centre, Panchsheel Park, New Delhi – 110 017, India
Penguin Group (NZ), 67 Apollo Drive, Rosedale, North Shore 0632, New Zealand
(a division of Pearson New Zealand Ltd)
Penguin Books (South Africa) (Pty) Ltd, 24 Sturdee Avenue, Rosebank, Johannesburg 2196, South Africa

Penguin Books Ltd, Registered Offices: 80 Strand, London WC2R 0RL, England

puffinbooks.com

First published in Great Britain by Longman Young Books 1966
Published in Puffin Books 1979
Published in this edition 2009
This edition produced for The Book People Ltd,
Hall Wood Avenue, Haydock, St Helens, WA11 9UL
1

Text copyright © Aingelda Ardizzone, 1966
Illustrations copyright © Edward Ardizzone, 1966
Introduction copyright © Julia Eccleshare, 2009
All rights reserved

The moral right of the copyright holder has been asserted

Set in 17.5/24pt Perpetua
Typeset by Palimpsest Book Production Limited, Grangemouth, Stirlingshire
Made and printed in England by Clays Ltd, St Ives plc

British Library Cataloguing in Publication Data
A CIP catalogue record for this book is available from the British Library

ISBN: 978-0-141-33698-5

www.greenpenguin.co.uk

Mixed Sources
Product group from well-managed
forests and other controlled sources
www.fsc.org Cert no. SA-COC-1592
© 1996 Forest Stewardship Council

Penguin Books is committed to a sustainable future
for our business, our readers and our planet.
The book in your hands is made from paper
certified by the Forest Stewardship Council.

INTRODUCTION

BY JULIA ECCLESHARE, SERIES EDITOR

Anyone who thinks dolls are dull will think again after reading this wonderful story of abandonment, survival and rescue. *The Little Girl and the Tiny Doll* is a celebration of believing, and it is wonderful to be reminded that dolls can be real, and that they are not inanimate or passive. Dolls *are* real if we believe in them and only the hardest of hearts could fail to do so after reading this story. No one can be indifferent to the fate of the tiny doll – a gentle creature who, nonetheless, has a determined and resourceful character. She makes the best of her surroundings among the boxes of frozen peas in the shop freezer. Dressed only in a shift, she survives the frosty floor, avoids the risk of being crushed by a box of fish fingers and dodges the giant hands that poke into her new home. Her life is a sad one: it is impossible not to feel sorry for her and to worry about how she will ever escape. But then help comes in the shape of the little girl . . .

Aingelda Ardizzone's endearing short story, so charming in its simplicity, has captured the hearts and imaginations of generations of young children. She has created a nostalgic world of childhood long ago, which is touched by something more modern – a deep freeze. Edward Ardizzone's delicate line drawings complement the text beautifully and evoke a whole, credible, if unlikely, world for the tiny doll: they make her existence as 'real' as it can possibly be. As a result, the tiny doll comes alive and I love watching her excitement, surprise and joy as she receives her new clothes and especially the moment when she cleverly makes a bed for herself. How cosy she looks tucked up under the brown-paper blanket!

Magical things can happen if we believe that they will. *The Little Girl and the Tiny Doll* makes that belief easy.

To Miss Irene Theobald

There was once a tiny doll who
belonged to a girl who did not care
for dolls so her life was very dull.

For a long time she lay forgotten
in a mackintosh pocket until one
rainy day when the girl was
out shopping.

The girl was following her
mother round a grocer's shop
when she put her hand in

her pocket and felt something hard. She took it out and saw it was the doll.

'Ugly old thing,' she said and quickly put it back again, as she thought, into her pocket.

But, in fact, it fell unnoticed into the
deep freeze container among the
frozen peas.

The tiny doll lay quite still for a
long time,

wondering what was to become of her.

She felt so sad, partly because
she did not like being called ugly
and partly because she was lost.

5

It was very cold in the deep freeze
and the tiny doll began to feel rather
stiff, so she decided to walk about
and have a good look at the place.

The floor was crisp and white
just like frost on a winter's morning.

6

There were many packets of peas
piled one on top of the other.
They seemed to her like great
big buildings. The cracks between
the piles were rather like
narrow streets.

She walked one way and then the
other, passing, not only packets of
peas, but packets of sliced beans,
spinach, broccoli and mixed
vegetables. Then she turned a corner

8

and found herself among beef
rissoles and fish fingers. However, she
did not stop but went on exploring
until she came to boxes of strawberries;
and then ice-cream.

The strawberries reminded her of
the time when she was lost once
before among the strawberry plants
in a garden.

Then she sat all day in the sun
smelling and eating strawberries.
   Now she made herself as
comfortable as possible.

But it was not easy as the customers
kept taking boxes out to buy them and

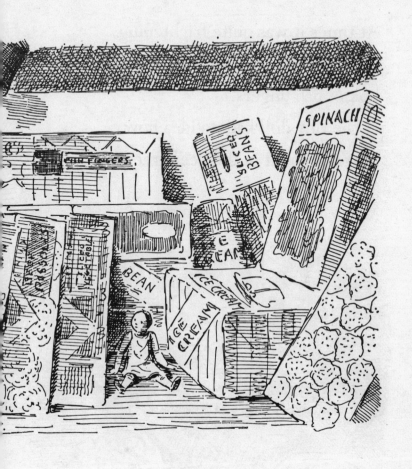

the shop people would put new ones in
and not always very carefully, either.

At times it was quite frightening.
Once she was nearly squashed by a
box of fish fingers.

The tiny doll had no idea how
long she spent in the deep freeze.

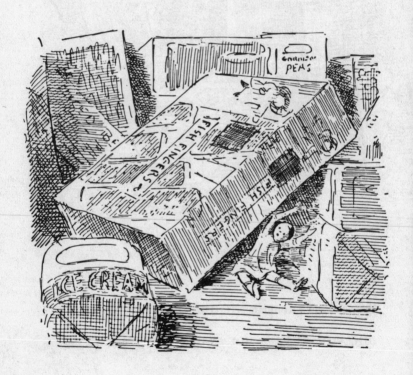

Sometimes it seemed very quiet.
This, she supposed, was when the
shop was closed for the night.

She could not keep count of the days.

One day when she was busy
eating ice-cream out of a packet,
she suddenly looked up and saw a
little girl she had never seen before.

The little girl was sorry for the tiny
doll and longed to take her home
to be with her other dolls.

The doll looked so cold and lonely,
but the girl did not dare to pick
her up because she had been told
not to touch things in the shop.

However, she felt she must do
something to help the doll and as
soon as she got home she set to
work to make her some warm clothes.

First of all, she made her a warm
bonnet out of a piece of red flannel.
This was a nice and easy thing to
start with.

After tea that day she asked mother
to help her cut out a coat from a
piece of blue velvet.

She stitched away so hard that
she had just time to finish it before
she went to bed.

It was very beautiful.

The next day her mother said they were going shopping, so the little girl put the coat and bonnet in an empty matchbox and tied it into a neat parcel with brown paper and string.

She held the parcel tightly in her
hand as she walked along
the street, hurrying as she went.
She longed to know if the tiny doll
would still be there.

As soon as she reached the shop
she ran straight to the deep freeze
to look for her.

At first she could not see her anywhere.
Then, suddenly, she saw her, right
at the back, playing with the peas.

The tiny doll was throwing them
into the air and hitting them with
an ice-cream spoon.

It was a very dull game but it was
something to do.

The little girl threw in the parcel and
the doll at once started to untie it.

She looked very pleased when she
saw what was inside.

She tried on the coat, and it fitted.
She tried on the bonnet and it fitted
too. She was very pleased.

She jumped up and down with
excitement and waved to the little
girl to say thank you.

She felt so much better in warm
clothes and it made her feel happy to
think that somebody cared for her.

Then she had an idea. She made
the matchbox into a bed and
pretended that the brown paper was
a great big blanket.

With the string she wove a mat to
go beside the bed.

At last she settled down in the
matchbox, wrapped herself in the
brown paper blanket and went to sleep.

She had a long, long sleep because she
was very tired and, when she woke up,
she found that the little girl had been

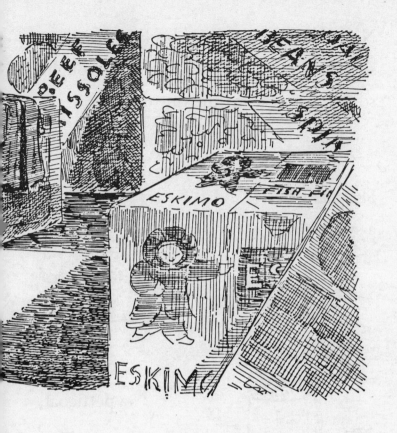

back again and had left another
parcel. This time it contained a yellow
scarf. She had always wanted a scarf.

Now the little girl came back to the
shop every day and each time she brought
something new for the tiny doll.

She made her
a sweater,

a petticoat,

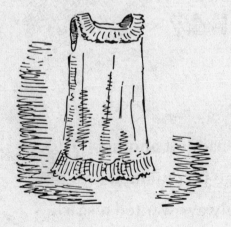

knickers with tiny frills,

and gave her a little bit of looking-
glass to see herself in.

She also gave her some red tights
which belonged to one of her own
dolls to see if they would fit. They
fitted perfectly.

At last the tiny doll was beautifully
dressed and looked quite cheerful,
but still nobody except the little girl
ever noticed her.

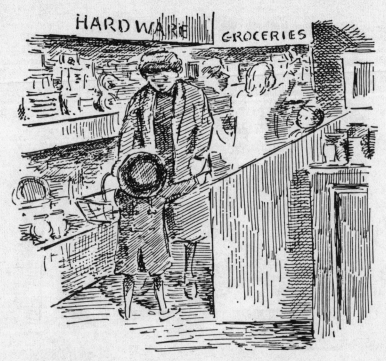

'Couldn't we ask someone about the
doll?' the little girl asked her mother.
'I would love to take her home to
play with.'

The mother said she would ask
the lady at the cash desk when they
went to pay for their shopping.

'Do you know about the doll in the
deep freeze?'

'No, indeed,' the lady replied.
'There are no dolls in this shop.'

39

'Oh yes there are,' said the little
girl and her mother, both at once.

So the lady from the cash desk, the
little girl and her mother all marched

off to have a look.

And there, sure enough, was the
tiny doll down among the frozen peas,
looking cold and bored.

'It's not much of a life for a doll in
there,' said the shop lady picking up
the doll and giving it to the little girl.
'You had better take her home
where she will be out of mischief.'

Having said this, she marched back
to her desk with rather a haughty
expression.

The little girl took the tiny doll
home, where she lived for many
happy years in a beautiful doll's
house. The little girl loved her and
played with her a great deal.

But, best of all, she liked the company
of the other dolls, because they
all loved to listen to her stories
about the time when she lived in
the deep freeze.

THE END

Milly-Molly-Mandy Stories

JOYCE LANKESTER BRISLEY

The enchanting and classic adventures of a little country girl, the Milly-Molly-Mandy stories are perfect for reading aloud. They have been loved and shared for over 75 years with their timeless sense of fun and beautiful detail.

Whether blackberry picking with Billy Blunt and little-friend-Susan or winning prizes at the village fête, Milly-Molly-Mandy continues to delight new readers and old friends alike!

Magical adventures in a bestselling series

Mr Majeika

When Mr Majeika is in charge, there are bound to be tricks in store for Class Three.

Mr Majeika – he's a wizard in the classroom.

Puffin by Post

The Little Girl and the Tiny Doll – Edward and Aingelda Ardizzone

If you have enjoyed this book and want to read more,
then check out these other great Puffin titles.
You can order any of the following books direct with Puffin by Post:

A Child's Christmas in Wales • Dylan Thomas/Edward Ardizzone • 9780140377231	£4.99
A magical account of Christmas Day in a small Welsh town	
George's Marvellous Medicine • Roald Dahl • 9780141323053	£4.99
A favourite classic Roald Dahl story	
The Worst Witch • Jill Murphy • 9780140372496	£4.99
The first in the hilarious Worst Witch series	
Mr Majeika • Humphrey Carpenter • 9780141323084	£4.99
Timeless adventures with everyone's favourite teacher	
Gobbolino The Witch's Cat • Ursula Moray Williams • 9780141323268	£5.99
Charming adventures of a cat who just wants to be ordinary	

Just contact:

Puffin Books, C/o Bookpost, PO Box 29,
Douglas, Isle of Man, IM99 1BQ
Credit cards accepted. For further details:
Telephone: 01624 677237
Fax: 01624 670923

You can email your orders to: bookshop@enterprise.net
Or order online at: www.bookpost.co.uk

Free delivery in the UK.
Overseas customers must add £2 per book.

Prices and availability are subject to change.

Visit puffin.co.uk to find out about the latest titles, read extracts and
exclusive author interviews, and enter exciting competitions.
You can also browse thousands of Puffin books online.